Robert L. Stevenson, William E. Henley

Macaire

a melodramatic farce

Robert L. Stevenson, William E. Henley

Macaire
a melodramatic farce

ISBN/EAN: 9783337332273

Printed in Europe, USA, Canada, Australia, Japan

Cover: Foto ©Andreas Hilbeck / pixelio.de

More available books at **www.hansebooks.com**

MACAIRE

A MELODRAMATIC FARCE

BY

ROBERT LOUIS STEVENSON

AND

WILLIAM ERNEST HENLEY

CHICAGO

STONE AND KIMBALL

MDCCCXCV

PERSONS REPRESENTED.

ROBERT MACAIRE.

BERTRAND.

DUMONT, Landlord of the *Auberge des Adrets*.

CHARLES, a Gendarme, Dumont's supposed son.

GORIOT.

THE MARQUIS, Charles's father.

THE BRIGADIER of Gendarmerie.

THE CURATE.

A WAITER.

ERNESTINE, Goriot's daughter.

ALINE.

MAIDS, PEASANTS (Male and Female), GENDARMES.

———

The Scene is laid in the Courtyard of the *Auberge des Adrets*, on the frontier of France and Savoy. The time, 1820. The Action occupies an interval of from twelve to fourteen hours: from four in the afternoon till about five in the morning.

———

NOTE. — The time between the Acts should be as brief as possible, and the piece played, where it is merely comic, in a vein of patter.

THE FIRST ACT.

MACAIRE.

THE FIRST ACT.

The Stage represents the Courtyard of the Auberge des
Adrets. It is surrounded with the buildings of the
inn, with a gallery on the first story, approached C.,
by a straight flight of stairs. L. C., the entrance door-
way. A little in front of this, a small grated office,
containing a business table, brass-bound cabinet, and
portable cash-box. In front, R. and L., tables and
benches: one, L., partially laid for a considerable
party.

SCENE I.

ALINE *and* MAIDS; *to whom* FIDDLERS; *afterwards* DUMONT *and* CHARLES. *As the curtain rises, the sound of the violin is heard
approaching.* ALINE *and the inn servants,
who are discovered laying the table, dance up
to door L. C., to meet the* FIDDLERS, *who enter*

3

likewise dancing to their own music. AIR :
"*Haste to the Wedding.*" *The* FIDDLERS
exeunt playing into house, R. U. E. ALINE *and*
MAIDS *dance back to table, which they proceed
to arrange.*

ALINE.

Well, give me fiddles : fiddles and a wedding feast. It tickles your heart till your
heels make a runaway match of it. I don't
mind extra work, I don't, so long as there's
fun about it. Hand me up that pile of
plates. The quinces there, before the
bride. Stick a pink in the Notary's glass :
that's the girl he's courting.

DUMONT.

(*Entering with* CHARLES.) Good girls,
good girls ! Charles, in ten minutes from
now what happy faces will smile around
that board !

CHARLES.

Sir, my good fortune is complete ; and
most of all in this, that my happiness has
made my father happy.

DUMONT.

Your father? Ah, well, upon that point we shall have more to say.

CHARLES.

What more remains that has not been said already? For surely, sir, there are few sons more fortunate in their father: and, since you approve of this marriage, may I not conceive you to be in that sense fortunate in your son?

DUMONT.

Dear boy, there is always a variety of considerations. But the moment is ill chosen for dispute ; to-night, at least, let our felicity be unalloyed. (*Looking off, L. C.*) Our guests arrive: here is our good Curate, and here our cheerful Notary.

CHARLES.

His old infirmity, I fear.

DUMONT.

But, Charles — dear boy ! — at your wed-

ding feast! I should have taken it un-
neighbourly had he come strictly sober.

Scene II.

To these, by the door, L. C., the Curate *and the*
Notary, *arm in arm, the latter owl-like and
titubant.*

CURATE.

Peace be on this house!

NOTARY.

(*Singing.*) "Prove an excuse for the
glass."

DUMONT.

Welcome, excellent neighbours! The
Church and the Law.

CURATE.

And you, Charles, let me hope your feelings are in solemn congruence with this
momentous step.

NOTARY.

(*Digging* CHARLES *in the ribs.*) Married?
Lovely bride? Prove an excuse!

DUMONT.

(*To* CURATE.) I fear our friend? perhaps? as usual? eh?

CURATE.

Possibly : I had not yet observed it.

DUMONT.

Well, well, his heart is good.

CURATE.

He doubtless meant it kindly.

NOTARY.

Where's Aline?

ALINE.

Coming, sir!   (NOTARY *makes for her.*)

CURATE.

(*Capturing him.*)   You will infallibly expose yourself to misconstruction.   (*To* CHARLES.)   Where is your commanding officer?

CHARLES.

Why, sir, we have quite an alert.   Information has been received from Lyons that the notorious malefactor, Robert Macaire, has broken prison, and the Brigadier is now scouring the country in his pursuit. I myself am instructed to watch the visitors to our house.

DUMONT.

That will do, Charles: you may go. (*Exit* CHARLES.) You have considered the case I laid before you?

NOTARY.

Considered a case?

DUMONT.

Yes, yes. Charles, you know, Charles. Can he marry? under these untoward and peculiar circumstances, can he marry?

NOTARY.

Now lemme tell you: marriage is a contract to which there are two contracting parties. That being clear, I am prepared to argue it categorically that your son

Charles—who, it appears, is not your son Charles — I am prepared to argue that one party to a contract being null and void, the other party to a contract cannot by law oblige the first party to constract or bind himself to any contract, except the other party be able to see his way clearly to constract himself with him. I dunno if I make myself clear?

DUMONT.

No.

NOTARY.

Now, lemme tell you: by applying justice of peace might possibly afford relief.

DUMONT.

But how?

NOTARY.

Ay, there's the rub.

DUMONT.

But what am I to do? He's not my son, I tell you: Charles is not my son.

NOTARY.

I know.

DUMONT.

Perhaps a glass of wine would clear him?

NOTARY.

That's what I want. (*They go out, L. U. E.*)

ALINE.

And now, if you've done deranging my table, to the cellar for the wine, the whole pack of you. (*Manet sola, considering table.*) There: it's like a garden. If I had as sweet a table for my wedding, I would marry the Notary.

SCENE III.

The Stage remains vacant. Enter, by door, L. C., MACAIRE, followed by BERTRAND with bundle; in the traditional costume.

MACAIRE.

Good! No police.

BERTRAND.

(*Looking off, L. C.*) Sold again!

MACAIRE.

This is a favoured spot, Bertrand; ten
minutes from the frontier; ten minutes
from escape. Blessings on that frontier
line! The criminal hops across, and lo!
the reputable man. (*Reading.*) "*Auberge
des Adrets*, by John Paul Dumont." A
table set for company; this is fate: Bertrand, are we the first arrivals? An office;
a cabinet; a cash box — aha! and a cash
box, golden within. A money-box is like
a Quaker beauty: demure without, but
what a figure of a woman! Outside gallery: an architectural feature I approve;
I count it a convenience both for love and
war: the troubadour — twang-twang; the
craftsman — (*Makes as if turning key.*)
The kitchen window: humming with cook-
ery; truffles before Jove! I was born for
truffles. Cock your hat: meat, wine, rest,
and occupation; men to gull, women to

fool, and still the door open, the great un-
bolted door of the frontier!

BERTRAND.

Macaire, I'm hungry.

MACAIRE.

Bertrand, excuse me, you are a sensu-
alist. I should have left you in the stone-
yard at Lyons, and written no passport but
my own. Your soul is incorporate with
your stomach. Am I not hungry, too?
My body, thanks to immortal Jupiter, is
but the boy that holds the kite-string; my
aspirations and designs swim like the kite
sky-high, and overlook an empire.

BERTRAND.

If I could get a full meal and a pound
in my pocket I would hold my tongue.

MACAIRE.

Dreams, dreams! We are what we are;
and what are we? Who are you? who
cares? Who am I? myself. What do

we come from? an accident. What's a
mother? an old woman. A father? the
gentleman who beats her. What is crime?
discovery. Virtue? opportunity. Politics?
a pretext. Affection? an affectation. Mo-
rality? an affair of latitude. Punishment?
this side of the frontier. Reward? the
other. Property? plunder. Business?
other people's money — not mine, by God!
and the end of life to live till we are
hanged.

BERTRAND.

Macaire, I came into this place with my
tail between my legs already, and hungry
besides; and then you get to flourishing,
and it depresses me worse than the chaplain in the jail.

MACAIRE.

What is a chaplain? A man they pay
to say what you don't want to hear.

BERTRAND.

And who are you after all? and what
right have you to talk like that? By what

I can hear, you've been the best part of your life in quod ; and as for me, since I've followed you, what sort of luck have I had ? Sold again ! A boose, a blue fright, and two years' hard labour, and the police hot foot after us even now.

MACAIRE.

What is life ? A boose and the police.

BERTRAND.

Of course, I know you're clever; I ad- mire you down to the ground, and I'll starve without you. But I can't stand it, and I'm off. Good-bye : good luck to you, old man ; and if you want the bundle ——

MACAIRE.

I am a gentleman of a mild disposition, and, I thank my maker, elegant manners ; but rather than be betrayed by such a thing as you are, with the courage of a hare, and the manners, by the Lord Harry, of a jumping-jack —— (*He shows his knife.*)

BERTRAND.

Put it up put it up: I'll do what you want.

MACAIRE.

What is obedience? Fear. So march straight, or look for mischief. It's not *bon ton*, I know, and far from friendly. But what is friendship? convenience. But we lose time in this amiable dalliance. Come, now, an effort of deportment: the head thrown back, a jaunty carriage of the leg; crook gracefully the elbow. Thus. 'Tis better. (*Calling.*) House, house here!

BERTRAND.

Are you mad? We haven't a brass farthing.

MACAIRE.

Now! — But before we leave!

Scene IV.

To these, Dumont.

DUMONT.

Gentlemen; what can a plain man do for your service?

MACAIRE.

My good man, in a roadside inn one cannot look for the impossible. Give one what small wine and what country fare you can produce.

DUMONT.

Gentlemen, you come here upon a most auspicious day, a red-letter day for me and my poor house, when all are welcome. Suffer me, with all delicacy, to inquire if you are not in somewhat narrow circumstances?

MACAIRE.

My good creature, you are strangely in error; one is rolling in gold.

BERTRAND.

And very hungry.

DUMONT.

Dear me; and on this happy occasion I had registered a vow that every poor traveller should have his keep for nothing, and a pound in his pocket to help him on his journey.

MACAIRE.

A pound in his pocket?

BERTRAND.

Keep for nothing?

Aside.

MACAIRE.

Bitten!

BERTRAND.

Sold again!

DUMONT.

I will send you what we have : poor fare, perhaps, for gentlemen like you.

Scene V.

MACAIRE, BERTRAND ; *afterwards* CHARLES, *who appears on the gallery and comes down.*

BERTRAND.

I told you so.   Why will you fly so high?

MACAIRE.

Bertrand, don't crush me.   A pound:

c

a fortune! With a pound to start upon — two pounds, for I'd have borrowed yours — three months from now I might have been driving in my barouche, and you behind it, Bertrand, in a tasteful livery.

BERTRAND.

(*Seeing* CHARLES.) Lord, a policeman!

MACAIRE.

Steady! What is a policeman? Justice's blind eye. (*To* CHARLES.) I think, sir, you are in the force?

CHARLES.

I am, sir, and it was in that character ——

MACAIRE.

Ah, sir, a fine service!

CHARLES.

It is, sir, and if your papers ——

MACAIRE.

You become your uniform. Have you a mother? Ah, well, well!

CHARLES.

My duty, sir ——

MACAIRE.

They tell me one Macaire — is not that his name, Bertrand? — has broken jail at Lyons?

CHARLES.

He has, sir, and it is precisely for that reason ——

MACAIRE.

Well, good-bye. (*Shaking* CHARLES *by the hand, and leading him towards the door, L. U. E.*) Sweet spot, sweet spot. The scenery is . . (*kisses his finger tips. Exit* CHARLES). And now, what is a policeman?

BERTRAND.

A bobby.

Scene VI.

MACAIRE, BERTRAND ; *to whom* ALINE *with tray ; and afterwards* MAIDS.

ALINE.

(*Entering with tray, and proceeding to lay table, L.*) My men, you are in better luck than usual. It isn't every day you go shares in a wedding feast.

MACAIRE.

A wedding? Ah, and you're the bride?

ALINE.

What makes you fancy that?

MACAIRE.

Heavens, am I blind?

ALINE.

Well, then, I wish I was.

MACAIRE.

I take you at the word: have me.

ALINE.

You will never be hanged for modesty.

MACAIRE.

Modesty is for the poor: when one is

rich and nobly born, 'tis but a clog. I love you. What is your name?

ALINE.

Guess again, and you'll guess wrong. (*Enter the other servants with wine baskets.*) Here, set the wine down. No, that is the old Burgundy for the wedding party. These gentlemen must put up with a different bin. (*Setting wine before* MACAIRE *and* BERTRAND, *who are at table, L.*)

MACAIRE.

(*Drinking.*) Vinegar, by the supreme Jove!

BERTRAND.

Sold again!

MACAIRE.

Now, Bertrand, mark me. (*Before the servants he exchanges the bottle for the one in front of* DUMONT'S *place at the head of the other table.*) Was it well done?

BERTRAND.

Immense.

MACAIRE.

(*Emptying his glass into* BERTRAND'S.)
There, Bertrand, you may finish that. Ha!
music?

Scene VII.

To these, from the inn, L. U. E., DUMONT,
CHARLES, *the* CURATE, *the* NOTARY *jigging:
from the inn, R. U. E.,* FIDDLERS *playing and
dancing; and through door L. C.,* GORIOT,
ERNESTINE, PEASANTS, *dancing likewise.* AIR:
"*Haste to the Wedding.*" *As the parties
meet, the music ceases.*

DUMONT.

Welcome, neighbours! welcome, friends!
Ernestine, here is my Charles, no longer
mine. A thousand welcomes. O the gay
day! O the auspicious wedding! (CHARLES,
ERNESTINE, DUMONT, GORIOT, CURATE,
and NOTARY *sit to the wedding feast;*
PEASANTS, FIDDLERS, *and* MAIDS, *grouped
at back, drinking from the barrel.*) O, I
must have all happy around me.

GORIOT.

Then help the soup.

DUMONT.

Give me leave. I must have all happy.
Shall these poor gentlemen upon a day
like this drink ordinary wine? Not so: I
shall drink it. (*To* MACAIRE, *who is just
about to fill his glass.*) Don't touch it,
sir! Aline, give me that gentleman's bottle and take him mine : with old Dumont's
compliments.

MACAIRE.

What?

BERTRAND.

Change the bottle?

MACAIRE.

Bitten!

BERTRAND.

Sold again.

} *Aside.*

DUMONT.

Yes, all shall be happy.

GORIOT.

I tell'ee, help the soup!

DUMONT.

(*Begins to help soup. Then, dropping ladle.*) One word: a matter of detail: Charles is not my son. (*All exclaim.*) O no, he is not my son. Perhaps, I should have mentioned it before.

CHARLES.

I am not your son, sir?

DUMONT.

O no, far from it.

GORIOT.

Then who the devil's son be he?

DUMONT.

O, I don't know. It's an odd tale, a romantic tale: it may amuse you. It was twenty years ago, when I kept the *Golden Head* at Lyons: Charles was left upon my doorstep in a covered basket, with sufficient money to support the child till he should come of age. There was no mark upon the linen, nor any clue but one: an unsigned letter from the father of the child, which he strictly charged me to preserve. It was to prove his identity: he, of course, would know its contents, and he only; so I keep it safe in the third compartment of my cash-box, with the ten thousand francs I've saved for his dowry. Here is the key; it's a patent key. To-day the poor boy is twenty-one, to-morrow to be married. I did perhaps hope the father would appear: there was a Marquis coming; he wrote me for a room; I gave him the best, Number Thirteen, which you have all heard of: I did hope it might be he, for a Marquis, you know, is always genteel. But no, you see. As for me, I take you all to witness I'm as innocent of him as the babe unborn.

MACAIRE.

Ahem! I think you said the linen bore an M?

DUMONT.

Pardon me: the markings were cut off.

MACAIRE.

True. The basket white, I think?

DUMONT.

Brown, brown.

MACAIRE.

Ah! brown — a whitey-brown.

GORIOT.

I tell 'ee what, Dumont, this is all very
well; but in that case, I'll be danged if he
gets my daater.   (*General consternation.*)

DUMONT.

O Goriot, let's have happy faces!

GORIOT.

Happy faces be danged!   I want to
marry my daater; I want your son.   But
who be this?   I don't know, and you don't
know, and he don't know.   He may be
anybody; by Jarge, he may be nobody!
(*Exclamations.*)

CURATE.

The situation is crepuscular.

ERNESTINE.

Father, and Mr. Dumont (and you too,
Charles), I wish to say one word.   You

gave us leave to fall in love; we fell in love; and as for me, my father, I will either marry Charles, or die a maid.

CHARLES.

And you, sir, would you rob me in one day of both a father and a wife?

DUMONT.

(*Weeping.*) Happy faces, happy faces!

GORIOT.

I know nothing about robbery; but she cannot marry without my consent, and that she cannot get.

DUMONT.

O dear, O dear!

ALINE.

What, spoil the wedding?

ERNESTINE.

O father!

CHARLES.

Sir, sir, you would not——

Together.

GORIOT

(*Exasperated.*) I wun't, and what's more I shan't.

NOTARY.

I donno if I make myself clear ?

DUMONT.

Goriot, do let's have happy faces !

GORIOT.

Fudge ! Fudge ! ! Fudge ! ! !

CURATE.

Possibly on application to this conscientious jurist, light might be obtained.

ALL.

The Notary ; yes, yes ; the Notary !

DUMONT.

Now, how about this marriage ?

NOTARY.

Marriage is a contract, to which there are two contracting parties, John Doe and

Richard Roe. I donno if I make myself clear?

Poor lamb!

Silence, my friend; you will expose yourself to misconstruction.

(*Taking the stage.*) As an entire stranger in this painful scene, you will permit a gentleman and a traveller to interject one word? There sits the young man, full, I am sure, of pleasing qualities ; here the young maiden, by her own confession bashfully consenting to the match ; there sits that dear old gentleman ; a lover of bright faces like myself, his own now dimmed with sorrow, and here — (may I be allowed to add?) — here sits this noble Roman, a father like myself, and like myself the slave of duty. Last you have me — Baron Henri-Frédéric de Latour de Main de la Tonnerre de Brest, the man of the world and the man of delicacy. I find you all — permit me the expression — gravelled. A marriage and an obstacle. Now, what is marriage? The union of two souls, and, what is possibly more romantic, the fusion of two dowries. What is an obstacle? the devil. And this obstacle? to me, as a man of family, the obstacle seems grave; but to me, as a man and a brother, what is it but a word. O my friend (*to* GORIOT), you whom I single out as the victim of the same noble failing with myself — of pride of birth, of pride of honesty — O my friend, reflect. Go now apart with your dishevelled daughter, your tearful son-in-law, and let their plaints constrain you. Believe me, when you come to die, you will recall with pride this amiable weakness.

GORIOT.

I shan't, and what's more I wun't. (CHARLES *and* ERNESTINE *lead him up stage, protesting. All rise, except* NOTARY.)

DUMONT.

(*Front R., shaking hands with* MACAIRE.)

Sir, you have a noble nature. (MACAIRE *picks his pocket.*) Dear me, dear me, and you are rich.

MACAIRE.

I own, sir, I deceived you : I feared some wounding offer, and my pride replied. But to be quite frank with you, you behold me here, the Baron Henri-Frédéric de Latour de Main de la Tonnerre de Brest, and between my simple manhood and the infinite these rags are all.

DUMONT.

Dear me, and with this noble pride, my gratitude is useless. For I, too, have delicacy : I understand you could not stoop to take a gift.

MACAIRE.

A gift ? a small one ? never !

DUMONT.

And I will never wound you by the offer.

MACAIRE.

Bitten.

BERTRAND.

Sold again.

Aside.

GORIOT.

(*Taking the stage.*)   But, look'ee here,
he can't marry.

MACAIRE.

Hey?

DUMONT.

Ah!

ALINE.

Heyday!

CURATE.

Wherefore?

ERNESTINE.

Oh!

CHARLES.

Ah!

Together.

GORIOT.

Not without his veyther's consent! And he hasn't got it; and what's more, he can't get it; and what's more, he hasn't got a veyther to get it from. It's the law of France.

ALINE.

Then the law of France ought to be ashamed of itself.

ERNESTINE.

O, couldn't we ask the Notary again?

CURATE.

Indubitably you may ask him.

MACAIRE.

Can't they marry?

DUMONT.

Can't he marry?

ALINE.

Can't she marry?

Together.

D

ERNESTINE.

Can't we marry?

CHARLES.

Can't I marry?   } *Together.*

GORIOT.

Bain't I right?

NOTARY.

Constracting parties.

CURATE.

Possibly to-morrow at an early hour he may be more perspicuous.

GORIOT.

Ay, before he've time to get at it.

NOTARY.

Unoffending jurisconsult overtaken by sorrow. Possibly by applying justice of peace might afford relief.

MACAIRE.

Bravo!

DUMONT.

Excellent!

CHARLES.

Let's go at once!

ALINE.

The very thing!

ERNESTINE.

Yes, this minute!

Together.

GORIOT.

I'll go. I don't mind getting advice, but I wun't take it.

MACAIRE.

My friends, one word: I perceive by your downcast looks that you have not recognised the true nature of your responsibility as citizens of time. What is care? impiety. Joy? the whole duty of man.

Here is an opportunity of duty it were sinful to forego. With a word, I could lighten your hearts; but I prefer to quicken your heels, and send you forth on your ingenuous errand with happy faces and smiling thoughts, the physicians of your own recovery. Fiddlers, to your catgut. Up, Bertrand, and show them how one foots it in society; forward, girls, and choose me every one the lad she loves; Dumont, benign old man, lead forth our blushing curate; and you, O bride, embrace the uniform of your beloved, and help us dance in your wedding-day. (*Dance, in the course of which* MACAIRE *picks* DUMONT'S *pocket of his keys, selects the key of the cash-box, and returns the others to his pocket. In the end, all dance out; the wedding-party, headed by* FIDDLERS, *L. C.; the* MAIDS *and* ALINE *into the inn, R. U. E. Manent* BERTRAND *and* MACAIRE.)

SCENE VIII.

MACAIRE, BERTRAND, *who instantly takes a bottle from the wedding-table, and sits with it, L.*

MACAIRE.

Bertrand, there's a devil of a want of a father here.

BERTRAND.

Ay, if we only knew where to find him.

MACAIRE.

Bertrand, look at me : I am Macaire ; I am that father.

BERTRAND.

You, Macaire ? you a father ?

MACAIRE.

Not yet : but in five minutes. I am capable of any thing. (*Producing key.*) What think you of this ?

BERTRAND.

That ? Is it a key ?

MACAIRE.

Ay, boy, and what besides ? my diploma
of respectability, my patent of fatherhood.
I prigged it — in the ardour of the dance I
prigged it ; I change it beyond recognition,
thus (*twists the handle of the key*); and now
. . . ?　Where is my long-lost child ? produce my young policeman, show me my
gallant boy.

BERTRAND.

I don't understand.

MACAIRE.

Dear innocence, how should you ?　Your
brains are in your fists.　Go and keep
watch.　(*He goes into the office and returns
with the cash-box.*)　Keep watch, I say.

BERTRAND.

Where ?

MACAIRE.

Everywhere.　(*He opens box.*)

BERTRAND.

Gold.

MACAIRE.

Hands off! Keep watch. (BERTRAND *at back of stage.*) Beat slower, my paternal heart! The third compartment; let me see.

BERTRAND.

S'st! (MACAIRE *shuts box.*) No; false alarm.

MACAIRE.

The third compartment. Aye, here it is ——— .

BERTRAND.

S'st! (*Same business.*) No: fire away.

MACAIRE.

The third compartment; it must be this.

BERTRAND.

S'st! (MACAIRE *keeps box open watching* BERTRAND.) All serene: it's the wind.

MACAIRE.

Now, see here! (*He darts his knife into the stage.*) I will either be backed as a

man should be, or from this minute out
I'll work alone. Do you understand? I
said alone.

BERTRAND.

For the Lord's sake, Macaire!———

MACAIRE.

Ay, here it is. (*Reading letter.*) "Preserve this letter secretly; its terms are
known only to you and me: hence, when
the time comes, I shall repeat them, and
my son will recognise his father." Signed:
"Your Unknown Benefactor." (*He hums
it over twice and replaces it. Then, finger-
ing the gold.*) Gold! The yellow enchant-
ress, happiness ready-made and laughing
in my face! Gold: what is gold? The
world; the term of ills; the empery of all;
the multitudinous babble of the 'change,
the sailing from all ports of freighted argo-
sies; music, wine, a palace; the doors of
the bright theatre, the key of consciences,
and love — love's whistle! All this below
my itching fingers; and to set this by, turn

a deaf ear upon the siren present, and con-
descend once more, naked, into the ring
with fortune — Macaire, how few would do
it ! But you, Macaire, you are compacted
of more subtile clay. No cheap immediate
pilfering ; no retail trade of petty larceny ;
but swoop at the heart of the position, and
clutch all !

BERTRAND.

(*At his shoulder.*) Halves !

MACAIRE.

Halves ? (*He locks the box.*) Bertrand,
I am a father. (*Replaces box in office.*)

BERTRAND.

(*Looking after him.*) Well, I — am —
damned !

DROP.

THE SECOND ACT.

THE SECOND ACT.

When the curtain rises, the night has come. A hanging cluster of lighted lamps over each table, R. and L. MACAIRE, E., smoking a cigarette; BERTRAND, L., with a churchwarden; each with bottle and glass.

SCENE I.

MACAIRE, BERTRAND.

MACAIRE.

Bertrand, I am content: a child might play with me. Does your pipe draw well?

BERTRAND.

Like a factory chimney. This is my notion of life: liquor, a chair, a table to put my feet on, a fine clean pipe, and no police.

MACAIRE.

Bertrand, do you see these changing exhalations? do you see these blue rings

and spirals, weaving their dance, like a
round of fairies, on the footless air?

BERTRAND.

I see 'em right enough.

MACAIRE.

Man of little visions, expound me these
meteors? what do they signify, O wooden-
head? Clod, of what do they consist?

BERTRAND.

Damned bad tobacco.

MACAIRE.

I will give you a little course of science.
Everything, Bertrand (much as it may surprise you), has three states: a vapour, a
liquid, a solid. These are fortune in the
vapour: these are ideas. What are ideas?
the protoplasm of wealth. To your head
— which, by the way, is a solid, Bertrand —
what are they but foul air? To mine, to
my prehensile and constructive intellects,
see, as I grasp and work them, to what

lineaments of the future they transform themselves : a palace, a barouche, a pair of luminous footmen, plate, wine, respect, and to be honest !

BERTRAND.

But what's the sense in honesty ?

MACAIRE.

The sense ? You see me : Macaire : elegant, immoral, invincible in cunning ; well, Bertrand, much as it may surprise you, I am simply damned by my dishonesty.

BERTRAND.

No !

MACAIRE.

The honest man, Bertrand, that God's noblest work. He carries the bag, my boy. Would you have me define honesty ? the strategic point for theft. Bertrand, if I'd three hundred a year, I'd be honest to-morrow.

BERTRAND.

Ah ! Don't you wish you may get it !

MACAIRE.

Bertrand, I will bet you my head against your own — the longest odds I can imagine — that with honesty for my springboard, I leap through history like a paper hoop, and come out among posterity heroic and immortal.

Scene II.

To these all the former characters, less the No-
TARY.   The fiddles are heard without, playing
dolefully.   Air: " O dear, what can the mat-
ter be?"   in time to which the procession
enters.

MACAIRE.

Well, friends, what cheer?

ALINE.

No wedding, no wedding!   *Together.*

GORIOT.

I told 'ee he can't, and he can't!

DUMONT.

Dear, dear me.

ERNESTINE.

They won't let us marry.

CHARLES.

No wife, no father, no noth-ing.

Together.

CURATE.

The facts have justified the worst antici-pations of our absent friend, the Notary.

MACAIRE.

I perceive I must reveal myself.

DUMONT.

God bless me, no!

MACAIRE.

My friends, I had meant to preserve a strict incognito, for I was ashamed (I own it!) of this poor accoutrement; but when I see a face that I can render happy, say, my

E

old Dumont, should I hesitate to make the change? Hear me, then, and you (*to the others*) prepare a smiling countenance. (*Repeating.*) "Preserve this letter secretly; its terms are only known to you and me; hence when the time comes, I shall repeat them, and my son will recognise his father. — Your Unknown Benefactor."

DUMONT.

The words! the letter! Charles, alas! it is your father!

CHARLES.

Good Lord! (*General consternation.*)

BERTRAND.

(*Aside: smiting his brow.*) I see it now; sublime!

CURATE.

A highly singular eventuality.

GORIOT.

Him? O well, then, I wun't. (*Goes up.*)

MACAIRE.

Charles, to my arms! (*Business.*) Ernestine, your second father waits to welcome you. (*Business.*) Goriot, noble old man, I grasp your hand. (*He doesn't.*) And you, Dumont, how shall your unknown benefactor thank you for your kindness to this boy? (*A dead pause.*) Charles, to my arms!

CHARLES.

My father, you are still something of a stranger. I hope — er — in the course of time — I hope that may be somewhat mended. But I confess that I have so long regarded Mr. Dumont —

MACAIRE.

Love him still, dear boy, love him still. I have not returned to be a burden on your heart, nor much, comparatively, on your pocket. A place by the fire, dear boy, a crust for my friend, Bertrand. (*A dead pause.*) Ah, well, this is a different home-coming from that I fancied when I

left the letter: I dreamed to grow rich.
Charles, you remind me of your sainted
mother.

CHARLES.

I trust, sir, you do not think yourself
less welcome for your poverty.

MACAIRE.

Nay, nay — more welcome, more wel-
come. O, I know your — (*business*) backs!
Besides, my poverty is noble. Political
. . . Dumont, what are your politics?

DUMONT.

A plain old republican, my lord.

MACAIRE.

And yours, my good Goriot?

GORIOT.

I be a royalist, I be, and so be my
daater.

MACAIRE.

How strange is the coincidence! The
party that I sought to found combined the

peculiarities of both: a patriotic enterprise in which I fell. This humble fellow ... have I introduced him? You behold in us the embodiment of aristocracy and democracy. Bertrand, shake hands with my family. (BERTRAND *is rebuffed by one and the other in dead silence.*)

BERTRAND.

Sold again!

MACAIRE.

Charles, to my arms! (*Business.*)

ERNESTINE.

Well, but now that he has a father of some kind, cannot the marriage go on?

MACAIRE.

Angel, this very night: I burn to take my grandchild on my knees.

GORIOT.

Be you that young man's veyther?

MACAIRE.

Ay, and what a father!

GORIOT.

Then all I've got to say is, I shan't and I wun't.

MACAIRE.

Ah, friends, friends, what a satisfaction it is, what a sight is virtue! I came among you in this poor attire to test you; how nobly have you born the test! But my disguise begins to irk me: who will lend me a good suit? (*Business.*)

Scene III.

To these, the Marquis, *L. C.*

MARQUIS.

Is this the house of John Paul Dumont, once of Lyons?

DUMONT.

It is, sir, and I am he, at your disposal.

MARQUIS.

I am the Marquis Villers-Cotterêts de la Cherté de Médoc. (*Sensation.*)

MACAIRE.

Marquis, delighted, I am sure.

MARQUIS.

(*To* DUMONT.) I come, as you perceive, unfollowed; my errand, therefore, is discreet. I come (*producing notes from breast pocket*) equipped with thirty thousand francs; my errand, therefore, must be generous. Can you not guess?

DUMONT.

Not I, my lord.

MARQUIS.

(*Repeating.*) "Preserve this letter," etc.

MACAIRE.

Bitten.

BERTRAND.

Sold again (*aside*). (*A pause.*)

ALINE.

Well, I never did!

DUMONT.

Two fathers !

MARQUIS.

Two ?   Impossible.

DUMONT.

Not at all.   This is the other.

MARQUIS.

This man ?

MACAIRE.

This is the man, my lord ; here stands the
father : Charles to my arms !   (CHARLES
backs.)

DUMONT.

He knew the letter.

MARQUIS.

Well, but so did I.

CURATE.

The judgment of Solomon.

GORIOT.

What did I tell 'ee ? he can't marry.

ERNESTINE.

Couldn't they both consent?

MARQUIS.

But he's my living image.

MACAIRE.

Mine, Marquis, mine.

MARQUIS.

My figure, I think?

MACAIRE.

Ah, Charles, Charles!

CURATE.

We used to think his physiognomy re-
sembled Dumont's.

DUMONT.

Come and look at him, he's really like
Goriot.

ERNESTINE.

O papa, I hope he's not my brother.

GORIOT.

What be talking of? I tell 'ee, he's like our Curate.

CHARLES.

Gentlemen, my head aches.

MARQUIS.

I have it: the involuntary voice of nature. Look at me, my son.

MACAIRE.

Nay, Charles, but look at me.

CHARLES.

Gentlemen, I am unconscious of the smallest natural inclination for either.

MARQUIS.

Another thought: what was his mother's name?

MACAIRE.

What was the name of his mother by you?

MARQUIS.

Sir, you are silenced.

MACAIRE.

Silenced by honour. I had rather lose my boy than compromise his sainted mother.

MARQUIS.

A thought: twins might explain it: had you not two foundlings?

DUMONT.

Nay, sir, one only; and judging by the miseries of this evening, I should say, thank God!

MACAIRE.

My friends, leave me alone with the Marquis. It is only a father that can understand a father's heart. Bertrand, follow the members of my family. (*They troop out, L. U. E. and R. U. E., the* FIDDLERS *playing.* AIR: "*O dear, what can the matter be?*")

Scene IV.

MACAIRE, MARQUIS.

MARQUIS.

Well, sir?

MACAIRE.

My lord, I feel for you.   (*Business.
They sit, R.*)

MARQUIS.

And now, sir?

MACAIRE.

The bond that joins us is remarkable
and touching.

MARQUIS.

Well, sir?

MACAIRE.

(*Touching him on the breast.*)   You have
there thirty thousand francs.

MARQUIS.

Well, sir?

MACAIRE.

I was but thinking of the inequalities of life, my lord : that I who, for all you know, may be the father of your son, should have nothing ; and that you who, for all I know, may be the father of mine, should be literally bulging with bank notes. . . . Where do you keep them at night?

MARQUIS.

Under my pillow. I think it rather ingenious.

MACAIRE.

Admirably so! I applaud the device.

MARQUIS.

Well, sir?

MACAIRE.

Do you snuff, my lord?

MARQUIS.

No, sir, I do not.

MACAIRE.

My lord, I am a poor man.

MARQUIS.

Well, sir, and what of that?

MACAIRE.

The affections, my lord, are priceless. Money will not buy them; or at least, it takes a great deal.

MARQUIS.

Sir, your sentiments do you honour.

MACAIRE.

My lord, you are rich.

MARQUIS.

Well, sir?

MACAIRE.

Now follow me, I beseech you. Here am I, my lord; and there, if I may so express myself, are you. Each has the father's heart, and there we are equal; each claims yon interesting lad, and there again we are on a par. But, my lord — and here we come to the inequality, and what I consider the unfairness of the thing

—you have thirty thousand francs, and I, my lord, have not a rap. You mark me? not a rap, my lord! My lord, put yourself in my position : consider what must be my feelings, my desires ; and — hey?

MARQUIS.

I fail to grasp . . .

MACAIRE.

(*With irritation.*) My dear man, there is the door of the house ; here am I ; there (*touching* MARQUIS *on the breast*) are thirty thousand francs. Well, now?

MARQUIS.

I give you my word and honour, sir, I gather nothing; my mind is quite unused to such prolonged exertion. If the boy be yours, he is not mine ; if he be mine, he is not yours ; and if he is neither of ours, or both of ours . . . in short, my mind . . .

MACAIRE.

My lord, will you lay those thirty thousand francs upon the table?

MARQUIS.

I fail to grasp . . . but if it will in any way oblige you . . . (*Does so.*)

MACAIRE.

Now, my lord, follow me: I take them up; you see? I put them in my pocket; you follow me? This is my hat; here is my stick; and here is my — my friend's bundle.

MARQUIS.

But that is my cloak.

MACAIRE.

Precisely. Now, my lord, one more effort of your lordship's mind. If I were to go out of that door, with the full intention — follow me close — the full intention of never being heard of more, what would you do?

MARQUIS.

I! — send for the police.

MACAIRE.

Take your money! (*Dashing down the*

notes.) Man, if I met you in a lane ! (*He drops his head upon the table.*)

MARQUIS.

The poor soul is insane. The other man whom I suppose to be his keeper, is very much to blame.

MACAIRE.

(*Raising his head.*) I have a light. (*To* MARQUIS.) With invincible owlishness, my lord, I cannot struggle. I pass you by ; I leave you gaping by the wayside ; I blush to have a share in the progeny of such an owl. Off, off, and send the tapster !

MARQUIS.

Poor fellow !

SCENE V.

MACAIRE, *to whom* BERTRAND. *Afterwards* DUMONT.

BERTRAND.

Well ?

MACAIRE.

Bitten.

F

BERTRAND.

Sold again.

MACAIRE.

Had he the wit of a lucifer match! But what can gods or men against stupidity? Still I have a trick. Where is that damned old man?

DUMONT.

(*Entering.*)   I hear you want me.

MACAIRE.

Ah, my good old Dumont, this is very sad.

DUMONT.

Dear me, what is wrong?

MACAIRE.

Dumont, you had a dowry for my son?

DUMONT.

I had; I have : ten thousand francs.

MACAIRE.

It's a poor thing, but it must do.   Dumont, I bury my old hopes, my old paternal tenderness.

DUMONT.

What, is he not your son?

MACAIRE.

Pardon me, my friend. The Marquis claims my boy. I will not seek to deny that he attempted to corrupt me, or that I spurned his gold. It was thirty thousand.

DUMONT.

Noble soul!

MACAIRE.

One has a heart . . . He spoke, Dumont, that proud noble spoke, of the advantages to our beloved Charles; and in my father's heart a voice arose, louder than thunder. Dumont, was I unselfish? The voice said no; the voice, Dumont, up and told me to begone.

DUMONT.

To begone? To go?

MACAIRE.

To begone, Dumont, and to go. Both, Dumont. To leave my son to marry, and be rich and happy as the son of another; to creep forth myself, old, penniless, broken-hearted, exposed to the inclemencies of heaven and the rebuffs of the police.

DUMONT.

This was what I had looked for at your hands. Noble, noble man!

MACAIRE.

One has a heart . . . And yet, Dumont, it can hardly have escaped your pene-tration that if I were to shift from this hostelry without a farthing, and leave my offspring to literally wallow among mil-lions, I should play the part of little better than an ass.

DUMONT.

But I had thought . . . I had fan-cied . . .

MACAIRE.

No, Dumont, you had not; do not seek to impose upon my simplicity. What you did think was this, Dumont: for the sake of this noble father, for the sake of this son whom he denies for his own interest — I mean, for his interest — no, I mean, for his own — well, anyway, in order to keep up the general atmosphere of sacrifice and nobility, I must hand over this dowry to the Baron Henri-Frédéric de Latour de Main de la Tonnerre de Brest.

DUMONT.

Noble, O noble!

Together: each shaking him by a hand.

BERTRAND.

Beautiful, O beautiful!

DUMONT.

Now Charles is rich he needs it not. For whom could it more fittingly be set aside than for his noble father? I will give it you at once.

BERTRAND.

At once, at once!

MACAIRE.

(*Aside to* BERTRAND.) Hang on. (*Aloud.*) Charles, Charles, my lost boy! (*He falls weeping at L. table.* DUMONT *enters the office, and brings down cash-box to table R. He feels in all his pockets:* BERTRAND, *from behind him, making signs to* MACAIRE, *which the latter does not see.*)

DUMONT.

That's strange. I can't find the key. It's a patent key.

BERTRAND.

(*Behind* DUMONT, *making signs to* MACAIRE.) The key, he can't find the key.

MACAIRE.

O yes, I remember. I heard it drop. (*Drops key.*) And here it is before my eyes.

DUMONT.

That? That's yours. I saw it drop.

MACAIRE.

I give you my word and honour I heard it fall five minutes back.

DUMONT.

But I saw it.

MACAIRE.

Impossible. It must be yours.

DUMONT.

It is like mine, indeed. How came it in your pocket?

MACAIRE.

Bitten. (*Aside.*)

BERTRAND.

Sold again (*aside*). . . . You forget, Baron, it's the key of my valise; I gave it to you to keep in consequence of the hole in my pocket.

MACAIRE.

True, true ; and that explains.

DUMONT.

O, that explains.   Now, all we have to
do is to find mine.   It's a patent key.   You
heard it drop ?

MACAIRE.

Distinctly.

BERTRAND.

So did I ; distinctly.

DUMONT.

Here, Aline, Babette, Goriot, Curate,
Charles, everybody, come here and look
for my key.

Scene VI.

*To these, with candles, all the former characters,
except* FIDDLERS, PEASANTS, *and* NOTARY. *They
hunt for the key.*

DUMONT.

It's bound to be here.   We all heard it
drop.

MARQUIS.

(*With* BERTRAND's *bundle.*)   Is this it ?

ALL.

(*With fury.*)   No.

BERTRAND.

Hands off, that's my luggage.   (*Hunt resumed.*)

DUMONT.

I heard it drop, as plain as ever I heard anything.

MARQUIS.

By the way (*all start up*) what are we looking for ?

ALL.

(*With fury.*)   O !!

DUMONT.

Will you have the kindness to find my key ?   (*Hunt resumed.*)

CURATE.

What description of a key ——

DUMONT.

A patent, patent, patent, patent key!

MACAIRE.

I have it. Here it is.

ALL.

(*With relief.*) Ah!!

DUMONT.

That? What do you mean? That's yours.

MACAIRE.

Pardon me.

DUMONT.

It is.

MACAIRE.

It isn't.

DUMONT.

I tell you, it is: look at that twisted handle.

MACAIRE.

It can't be mine, and so it must be yours.

DUMONT.

It is NOT. Feel in your pockets. (*To the others.*) Will you have the kindness to find my patent key?

ALL.

Oh!! (*Hunt resumed.*)

MACAIRE.

Ah, well, you're right. (*He slips key into* DUMONT'S *pocket.*) An idea: suppose you felt in your pocket?

ALL.

(*Rising.*) Yes! Suppose you did!

DUMONT.

I will not feel in my pockets. How could it be there? It's a patent key. This is more than any man can bear. First, Charles is one man's son, and then he's another's, and then he's nobody's, and be damned to him! And then there's my key lost; and then there's your key! What is your key? Where is your key? Where isn't it? And why is it like mine, only mine's a patent? The long and short of it is this: that I'm going to bed, and that you're all going to bed, and that I refuse to hear another word upon that subject or upon any subject. There!

MACAIRE.

Bitten.

BERTRAND.

Sold again.

Aside.

(ALINE *and* MAIDS *extinguish hanging lamps over tables, R. and L. Stage lighted only by guests' candles.*)

CHARLES.

But, sir, I cannot decently retire to rest until I embrace my honoured parent. Which is it to be?

MACAIRE.

Charles, to my ——

DUMONT.

Embrace neither of them; embrace no-body; there has been too much of this sickening folly. To bed!!! (*Exit violently R. U. E. All the characters troop slowly up stairs, talking in dumb show.* BERTRAND *and* MACAIRE *remain in front, C., watching them go.*)

BERTRAND.

Sold again, captain?

MACAIRE.

Ay, they will have it.

BERTRAND.

It? What?

MACAIRE.

The worst, Bertrand. What is man? — a beast of prey. An hour ago, and I'd have taken a crust, and gone in peace.

But no: they would trick and juggle, curse them; they would wiggle and cheat! Well, I accept the challenge: war to the knife.

BERTRAND.

Murder?

MACAIRE.

What is murder? A legal term for a man dying. Call it Fate, and that's philosophy; call me Providence, and you talk religion. Die? Why, that is what man is made for; we are full of mortal parts; we are all as good as dead already, we hang so close upon the brink: touch but a button, and the strongest falls in dissolution. Now, see how easy: I take you —— (*grappling him*).

BERTRAND.

Macaire — O no!

MACAIRE.

Fool! would I harm a fly; when I had nothing to gain? As the butcher with

the sheep, I kill to live; and where is the
difference between man and mutton? pride
and a tailor's bill? Murder? I know who
made that name — a man crouching from
the knife! Selfishness made it — the ag-
gregated egotism called society; but I
meet that with a selfishness as great.
Has he money? Have I none — great
powers, none? Well, then, I fatten and
manure my life with his.

BERTRAND.

You frighten me. Who is it?

MACAIRE.

Mark well. (*The* MARQUIS *opens the
door of Number Thirteen, and the rest, clus-
tering round, bid him good-night. As they
begin to disperse along the gallery he enters,
and shuts the door.*) Out, out, brief candle!
That man is doomed.

DROP.

THE THIRD ACT.

THE THIRD ACT.

SCENE I.

MACAIRE, BERTRAND.

*As the curtain rises, the stage is dark and empty.
Enter* MACAIRE *L. U. E., with lantern. He
looks about.*

MACAIRE.

(*Calling off.*)   S'st!

BERTRAND.

(*Entering L. U. E.*)   It's creeping dark.

MACAIRE.

Blinding dark; and a good job.

BERTRAND.

Macaire, I'm cold; my very hair's cold.

83

MACAIRE.

Work, work will warm you: to your keys.

BERTRAND.

No, Macaire, it's a horror. You'll not kill him; let's have no bloodshed.

MACAIRE.

None: it spoils your clothes. Now, see: you have keys, and you have experience: up that stair, and pick me the lock of that man's door. Pick me the lock of that man's door.

BERTRAND.

May I take the light?

MACAIRE.

You may not. Go. (BERTRAND *mounts the stairs, and is seen picking the lock of Number Thirteen.*) The earth spins eastward, and the day is at the door. Yet half-an-hour of covert, and the sun will be afoot, the discoverer, the great policeman. Yet half-an-hour of night, the good, hiding, practicable night; and lo! at a touch the gas-jet of the universe turned on; and up with the sun gets the providence of honest people, puts off his night-cap, throws up his window, stares out of house — and the rogue must skulk again till dusk. Yet, half-an-hour and, Macaire, you shall be safe and rich? If yon fool — my fool — would but miscarry, if the dolt within would hear and leap upon him, I could intervene, kill both, by heaven — both! — cry murder with the best, and at one stroke reap honour and gold. For, Bertrand dead ——

BERTRAND.

(*From above.*) S'st, Macaire!

MACAIRE.

Is it done, dear boy? Come down. (BER-TRAND *descends.*) Sit down beside this light: this is your ring of safety, budge not beyond — the night is crowded with hobgob-lins. See ghosts and tremble like a jelly if you must; but remember men are my con-

cern ; and at the creak of a man's foot, hist !
(*Sharpening his knife upon his sleeve.*)
What is a knife ?   A plain man's sword.

BERTRAND.

Not the knife, Macaire; O, not the
knife !

MACAIRE.

My name is Self-Defence.   (*He goes up
stairs and enters Number Thirteen.*)

BERTRAND.

He's in. I hear a board creak. What a
night, what a night ! Will he hear him ! O
Lord, my poor Macaire ! I hear nothing,
nothing. The night's as empty as a dream :
he must hear him : he cannot help but hear
him; and then — O Macaire, Macaire, come
back to me. It's death, and it's death, and
it's death. Red, red : a corpse. Macaire
to kill, Macaire to die ? I'd rather starve,
I'd rather perish, than either : I'm not fit,
I'm not fit, for either ! Why, how's this ?
I want to cry. (*A stroke, and a groan,*

from above.) God Almighty, one of them's gone! (*He falls, with his head on table, R.* MACAIRE *appears at the top of the stairs, descends, comes airily forward, and touches him on the shoulder.* BERTRAND, *with a cry, turns and falls upon his neck.*) O, O, and I thought I had lost him! (*Day breaking.*)

MACAIRE.

The contrary, dear boy. (*He produces notes.*)

BERTRAND.

What was it like?

MACAIRE.

Like? Nothing. A little blood, a dead man.

BERTRAND.

Blood! ... Dead! (*He falls at table sobbing.* MACAIRE *divides the notes into two parts; on the smaller he wipes the bloody knife, and folding the stains inward, thrusts the notes into* BERTRAND'S *face.*)

MACAIRE.

What is life without the pleasure of the table !

BERTRAND.

(*Taking and pocketing notes.*) Macaire, I can't get over it.

MACAIRE.

My mark is the frontier, and at top speed. Don't hang your jaw at me. Up, up, at the double ; pick me that cash-box ; and let's get the damned house fairly cleared.

BERTRAND.

I can't.   Did he bleed much ?

MACAIRE.

Bleed ?   Must I bleed you ?   To work, or I'm dangerous.

BERTRAND.

It's all right, Macaire ; I'm going.

MACAIRE.

Better so: an old friend is nearly sacred. (*Full daylight: lights up.* MACAIRE *blows out lantern.*)

BERTRAND.

Where's the key?

MACAIRE.

Key? I tell you to pick it.

BERTRAND.

(*With the box.*) But it's a patent lock. Where is the key? You had it.

MACAIRE.

Will you pick that lock?

BERTRAND.

I can't: it's a patent. Where's the key?

MACAIRE.

If you will have it, I put it back in that old ass's pocket.

BERTRAND.

Bitten, I think. (MACAIRE *dancing mad.*)

Scene II.

To these, DUMONT.

DUMONT.

Ah, friends, up so early? Catching the worm, catching the worm?

MACAIRE.

Good morning, good morning!

BERTRAND.

Early birds, early birds. (*Both sitting on the table and dissembling box.*)

DUMONT.

By the way, very remarkable thing: I found that key.

MACAIRE.

No?

BERTRAND.

O!

DUMONT.

Perhaps a still more remarkable thing :
it was my key that had the twisted handle.

MACAIRE.

I told you so.

DUMONT.

Now what we have to do is to get the
cash-box. Hallo! what's that you're sitting on?

BERTRAND.

Nothing.

MACAIRE.

The table! I beg your pardon.

DUMONT.

Why, it's my cash-box !

MACAIRE.

Why, so it is !

DUMONT.

It's very singular.

MACAIRE.

Diabolishly singular.

BERTRAND.

Early worms, early worms.

DUMONT.

(*Blowing in key.*) Well, I suppose you are still willing to begone?

MACAIRE.

More than willing, my dear soul: pressed, I may say, for time; for though it had quite escaped my memory, I have an appointment in Turin with a lady of title.

DUMONT.

(*At box.*) It's very odd. (*Blows in key.*) It's a singular thing (*blowing*), key won't turn. It's a patent key. Some one must have tampered with the lock (*blowing*). It's strangely singular, it's singularly singular! I've shown this key to commercial gentlemen all the way from Paris: they never saw a better key! (*more business*).

Well (*giving it up, and looking reproach-fully on key*), that's pretty singular.

MACAIRE.

Let me try. (*He tries, and flings down the key with a curse.*) Bitten.

BERTRAND.

Sold again.

DUMONT.

(*Picking up key.*) It's a patent key.

MACAIRE.

(*To* BERTRAND.) The game's up: we must save the swag. (*To* DUMONT.) Sir, since your key, on which I invoke the blight of Egypt, has once more defaulted, my feelings are unequal to a repetition of yesterday's distress, and I shall simply pad the hoof. From Turin you shall receive the address of my banker, and may prosperity attend your ventures. (*To* BERTRAND.) Now, boy! (*To* DUMONT.) Embrace my fatherless child: farewell!

(MACAIRE *and* BERTRAND *turn to go off, and are met in the door by the* GENDARMES.)

SCENE III.

To these, the BRIGADIER *and* GENDARMES.

BRIGADIER.

Let no man leave the house.

MACAIRE.

Bitten.

BERTRAND.

Sold again.

} *Aside.*

DUMONT.

Welcome, old friend !

BRIGADIER.

It is not the friend that comes ; it is the Brigadier. Summon your guests : I must investigate their passports. I am in pursuit of a notorious malefactor Robert Macaire.

DUMONT.

But I was led to believe that both Macaire and his accomplice had been arrested and condemned.

BRIGADIER.

They were, but they have once more escaped for the moment, and justice is indefatigable. (*He sits at table R.*) Dumont, a bottle of white wine.

MACAIRE.

(*To* DUMONT.) My excellent friend, I will discharge your commission and return with all speed. (*Going.*)

BRIGADIER.

Halt!

MACAIRE.

(*Returning: as if he saw* BRIGADIER *for the first time.*) Ha? a member of the force? Charmed, I'm sure. But you misconceive me: I return at once, and my friend remains behind to answer for me.

BRIGADIER.

Justice is insensible to friendship. I
shall deal with you in due time. Dumont,
that bottle.

MACAIRE.

Sir, my friend and I, who are students
of character, would grasp the opportunity
to share and — may one add? — to pay
the bottle. Dumont, three!

BERTRAND.

For God's sake! (*Enter* ALINE *and*
MAIDS.)

MACAIRE.

My friend is an author ; so, in a humbler
way, am I. Your knowledge of the criminal classes naturally tempts one to pursue
so interesting an acquaintance.

BRIGADIER.

Justice is impartial. Gentlemen, your
health.

MACAIRE.

Will not these brave fellows join us?

BRIGADIER.

They are on duty; but what matters?

MACAIRE.

My dear sir, what is duty? duty is my eye.

BRIGADIER.

(*Solemnly.*) And Betty Martin. (GEN-DARMES *sit at table.*)

MACAIRE.

(*To* BERTRAND.) Dear friend, sit down.

BERTRAND.

(*Sitting down.*) O Lord!

BRIGADIER.

(*To* MACAIRE.) You seem to be a gentleman of considerable intelligence.

MACAIRE.

I fear, sir, you flatter. One has lived, one has loved, and one remembers: that is all. One's *Lives of Celebrated Criminals*

H

have met with a certain success, and one is ever in quest of fresh material.

DUMONT.

By the way, a singular thing about my patent key.

BRIGADIER.

This gentleman is speaking.

MACAIRE.

Excellent Dumont! he means no harm. This Macaire is not personally known to you?

BRIGADIER.

Are you connected with justice?

MACAIRE.

Ah, sir, justice is a point above a poor author.

BRIGADIER.

(*With glass.*) Justice is the very devil.

MACAIRE.

My dear sir, my friend and I, I regret to say, have an appointment in Lyons, or I could spend my life in this society. Charge your glasses : one hour to madness and to joy! What is to-morrow? the enemy of to-day? Wine? the bath of life. One moment : I find I have forgotten my watch. (*He makes for the door.*)

BRIGADIER.

Halt !

MACAIRE.

Sir, what is this jest ?

BRIGADIER.

Sentry at the door. Your passports.

MACAIRE.

My good man, with all the pleasure in life. (*Gives papers. The* BRIGADIER *puts on spectacles, and examines them.*)

BERTRAND.

(*Rising, and passing round to* MACAIRE'S

other side.)   It's life and death : they must
soon find it.

MACAIRE.

(*Aside.*)   Don't I know?   My heart's
like fire in my body.

BRIGADIER.

Your name is ?

MACAIRE.

It is ; one's name is not unknown.

BRIGADIER.

Justice exacts your name.

MACAIRE.

Henri-Frédéric de Latour de Main de la
Tonnerre de Brest.

BRIGADIER.

Your profession ?

MACAIRE.

Gentleman.

BRIGADIER.

No, but what is your trade?

MACAIRE.

I am an analytical chymist.

BRIGADIER.

Justice is inscrutable. Your papers are in order. (*To* BERTRAND.) Now, sir, and yours?

BERTRAND.

I feel kind of ill.

MACAIRE.

Bertrand, this gentleman addresses you. He is not one of us: in other scenes, in the gay and giddy world of fashion, one is his superior. But to-day he represents the majesty of law; and as a citizen it is one's pride to do him honour.

BRIGADIER.

Those are my sentiments.

BERTRAND.

I beg your pardon, I —— (*Gives papers.*)

BRIGADIER.

Your name ?

BERTRAND.

Napoleon.

BRIGADIER.

What ? In your passport it is written Bertrand.

BERTRAND.

It's this way : I was born Bertrand, and then I took the name of Napoleon, and I mostly always call myself either Napoleon or Bertrand.

BRIGADIER.

The truth is always best.   Your profession ?

BERTRAND.

I am an orphan.

BRIGADIER.

What the devil! (*To* MACAIRE.) Is your friend an idiot?

MACAIRE.

Pardon me, he is a poet.

BRIGADIER.

Poetry is a great hindrance to the ends of justice. Well, take your papers.

MACAIRE.

Then we may go?

Scene IV.

To these CHARLES, *who is seen on the gallery, going to the door of Number Thirteen. Afterwards all the characters but the* NOTARY *and the* MARQUIS.

BRIGADIER.

One glass more. (BERTRAND *touches* MACAIRE, *and points to* CHARLES, *who enters Number Thirteen.*)

MACAIRE.

No more, no more, no more.

BRIGADIER.

(*Rising and taking* MACAIRE *by the arm.*)
I stipulate.

MACAIRE.

Engagement in Turin !

BRIGADIER.

Turin ?

MACAIRE.

Lyons, Lyons !

BERTRAND.

For God's sake. . . .

BRIGADIER.

Well, good-bye !

MACAIRE.

Good-bye, good ——

CHARLES.

(*From within.*) Murder! Help! (*Appearing.*) Help here! The Marquis is murdered.

BRIGADIER.

Stand to the door. A man up there. (*A* GENDARME *hurries up staircase into Number Thirteen,* CHARLES *following him. Enter on both sides of gallery the remaining characters of the piece, except the* NOTARY *and the* MARQUIS.)

MACAIRE.

Bitten, by God!

Aside.

BERTRAND.

Lost!

BRIGADIER.

(*To* DUMONT.) John Paul Dumont, I arrest you.

DUMONT.

Do your duty, officer. I can answer for myself and my own people.

BRIGADIER.

Yes, but these strangers?

DUMONT.

They are strangers to me.

MACAIRE.

I am an honest man : I stand upon my
rights : search me; or search this person,
of whom I know too little. (*Smiting his
brow.*) By heaven, I see it all. This morning —— (*To* BERTRAND.) How, sir, did
you dare to flaunt your booty in my very
face? (*To* BRIGADIER.) He showed me
notes ; he was up ere day ; search him, and
you'll find. There stands the murderer.

BERTRAND.

O, Macaire! (*He is seized and searched,
and the notes are found.*)

BRIGADIER.

There is blood upon the notes. Hand-
cuffs. (MACAIRE *edging toward the door.*)

BERTRAND.

Macaire, you may as well take the bundle.
(MACAIRE *is stopped by* SENTRY, *and comes front, R.*)

CHARLES.

(*Re-appearing.*) Stop, I know the truth.
(*He comes down.*) Brigadier, my father is not dead, he is not even dangerously hurt. He has spoken. There is the would-be assassin.

MACAIRE.

Hell! (*He darts across to the staircase, and turns on the second step, flashing out the knife.*) Back, hounds! (*He springs up the stair, and confronts them from the top.*) Fools, I am Robert Macaire! (*As* MACAIRE *turns to flee, he is met by the* GENDARME *coming out of Number Thirteen; he stands an instant checked, is shot from the stage, and falls headlong backward down the stair.* BERTRAND, *with a cry, breaks from the* GENDARMES, *kneels at his side, and raises his head.*)

BERTRAND.

Macaire, forgive me. I didn't blab ; you know I didn't blab.

MACAIRE.

Sold again, old boy. Sold for the last time ; at least, the last time this side death. Death, what is death ? (*He dies.*)

CURTAIN.

PRINTED AT THE NORWOOD PRESS
NORWOOD MASSACHUSETTS FOR
STONE AND KIMBALL PUBLISHERS
CHICAGO   MDCCCXCV